WINTER
Whirlwind

THE SUMMER UNPLUGGED SERIES

For my readers, who care about Jace and Bayleigh as much as I do.
This one is for you.

CHAPTER 1

A mountain of boxes leer at me in the dark room. I run my hand along the wall, looking for the light switch. I know it's here somewhere . . . I can't believe it's taking so long to get used to a new house. Finding the switch, finally, I flip on the light and immediately wish I could turn it back off again.

There are so many boxes.

I blow a raspberry with my tongue and venture through the foyer and into the living room of my brand new house. Jace and I had picked the floorplan and chosen everything from the paint color on the walls to the types of light switch covers that are in each room. And I still can't find the freaking switches, even after an entire week of living here.

Our living room, though big enough to house all of the new furniture we purchased, is currently being swallowed whole by all of the boxes we moved in here. It probably wasn't a good idea to buy new stuff and move in the old stuff at the same time. But my step-dad, David and Jace's dad, Gary had both been in town to celebrate our new house being finished and they wanted to help us move. We'd be stupid to say no to free moving help. But as it is now, hardly anything is unpacked.

Why? Because I suck.

I smile to myself and venture into the kitchen, my glorious kitchen. We have gorgeous hand-cut stone tile flooring, dark granite countertops and white cabinets that are all empty except for the one shelf that has Jett's plastic toddler plates, bowls, and sippy cups. The kitchen is my favorite room of the house. It's immaculate, has a massive kitchen island-bar-thing, and is perfect for entertaining. Now all I need to do is learn how to cook and I'll be throwing badass dinner parties in no time.

Although we moved in a week ago, everything is still a huge mess because we've been ridiculously busy at The Track. Last summer, I dove head first into Jace's dream—starting a motocross business. It took a lot of hard work getting the track designed and built, but the business has been up and running for a few months now. His best friend Park, who is also my best friend Becca's boyfriend, is our business partner. We split everything fifty/fifty, from the business decisions to the money to who has to deal with annoying parents of clients.

The Track is practically our second home. It's fun most of the time. We had planned for just a handful of clients when we first opened, and that ended up being a ridiculous understatement. Jace's first five clients turned into ten by the second day, and then twenty and now we're at a hundred and seven paying clients. Park has his own clients as well, and together, the boys are raking in cash at record levels. I am so proud of Jace, and in a weird way, proud of myself as well.

I finally feel like I have a purpose in this little family I share with Jace and our two-year-old, Jett. I have the job description of secretary, receptionist, social media coordinator, accounts payable, payroll, pizza delivery orderer, and my favorite title of all: the owner's wife.

Becca helps out a lot, although she's not an official salaried employee or anything. Her Etsy shop of handmade art has taken off and it's now her main job. But when she's not busy with that or college classes, she's hanging out with me at the Track. She and Park have been together two years now and we're all wondering when he's going to break down and propose already. I mean damn.

Anyhow, I make the precarious journey through the towers of boxes and get to the fridge to grab a soda. I'd left the Track earlier than Jace because he still had some work left to finish up. He'd kindly offered to keep the kiddo so I could get a shower without worrying about him for a while. I stub my toe on a box marked POTS AND PANS and vow to empty out the boxes this weekend. I can't keep living in the chaos of all of our crap. You can't even tell how pretty our new house is with all of these boxes in here.

On the way to the master bedroom, I stop by Jett's room. It's the only room in the house that's fully unpacked. When I'd taken Jett in to get his next round of booster shots at the doctor, I'd skimmed through a parenting magazine. Normally I don't give a shit about what people have to say on parenting, because in my opinion, parenting is an intuition. No one knows better for my kid than myself. However, in this one article I read about how the best way to handle moving houses with a kid is to pack up their room last and unpack it first in the new home. It said children can get nervous and scared in a new house and if things in their room go back to normal soon, it'll help them adjust. So that's exactly what I did.

I turn on the light and lean against the door frame, admiring my little man's room. It's fully dirt bike themed, thanks to Jace's insistence. Three of the walls are grey and one wall we painted in a black and white checkerboard pattern. Jace likes to joke that one day his son will be winning races and he'll get very used to seeing the checkered flag waving across the finish line. Then, with Becca's help, she and I painted these massive letters that spell out Jett's name and hung them on the wall. They're red and have tire marks painted in brown, making it look like they were run over by a motorcycle. It's pretty cute, and Jett seems to love it.

He still has a crib for now, but when he's old enough we plan to get him a bunk bed. His stuffed animals are lined up on the bed and his toys are organized along the opposite wall. I draw in a deep breath and enjoy the normalcy of Jett's room. It's a sanctuary in a house full of chaos. It's all neat and tidy and one day, the rest of the house will be just as clean.

I hope.

My phone buzzes, making me open my eyes. I'm still in Jett's room like some kind of dork, but hanging out in here makes me calm. As soon as I step back into the Boxes of Doom, I'll be annoyed again. I pull my phone out of my purse.

Jace: *I'm taking the kiddo to Magic Mark's Pizza. Want me to bring you back anything?*

My nose wrinkles as I type out a reply. *No thanks. I'm sick of pizza.*

Jace: *Want me to bring you anything from anywhere else?*

Me: *Nah, I'm okay.*

Jace: You sure? There's no food in the house.

Me: We have cereal. I'll eat some of that

Honestly at this point, I'm just so exhausted from the day that I don't mind eating some Cheerios and then passing out for the night. But Jace clearly isn't having that.

Jace: No, you need real food. I'm bringing you real food…but it'll be like an hour. Love you.

I roll my eyes and reply *love you, too*

An entire hour to myself? Nice. I head into our

room and close the bedroom door. I know I'm alone in the house but it's just weird getting naked with doors open. I walk over to Jace's laptop, which is one of the only things unpacked in our room and I blast some music, turning up the volume as loud as it'll go.

If our kitchen is my favorite part of the new house, our master bathroom is a close second. The bathroom is bigger than our old master room in the apartment we used to live in. It's separated into two areas, with two sinks and two closets for Jace and me. We have granite counters, lots of storage space, a built in makeup vanity, and a huge hot tub in the center of the room. On the opposite side of the room is a walk-in shower with glass walls. The shower is so huge you could live in it. There's two shower heads that pour from the ceiling, which makes it fun to take a shower with Jace in here. There's never a chance of running out of hot water, or not having enough space.

I turn on the water and step into the shower, reveling in the soothing hot water on my skin. It's been a long freaking day. It started with waking up at five in the morning and getting Jett dressed despite his best efforts to kick off anything I tried to put on him. Then I headed to the Track only to find that our printer had broken and it was invoice day. Then when it was finally fixed, we had a ton of people come in just to look around; kids who begged their parents to sign them up for lessons, local business owners coming by to say hello, other riders just checking out the place.

From the moment I got to work until right now, I've been busy as hell. And now I finally have some time alone. I can only hear a little of the music over the roar of the shower head, so I hum along while I shampoo my hair and close my eyes, letting the hot water wash away the stresses of the day.

A flicker of something gets my attention. I open my eyes and turn around, seeing nothing out of the ordinary in my bathroom. The glass shower walls are foggy and steam rolls through the air, but . . . I had to have imagined that . . . right?

I draw in a deep breath and go back to showering. And then it happens again. A shadow, a dark cloud crossing in front of the bathroom door, so quickly I almost miss it. Chills trickle down my back and a chill hits me, even under the hot water.

What the hell was that?

The shadow passes by the doorway again. I freeze. It was definitely human-shaped, not a figment of my imagination. Oh my god. Oh no. No no no.

Panic consumes me. The roar of the shower and the tinny blast of music from Jace's computer makes it impossible to hear anything. There's an intruder in my house and I'm freaking naked, in the shower, with no weapons or cell phone.

This is so not happening.

When the shadow walks by again, I realize whoever is in here hasn't come into the bathroom yet. He's walking around my room, probably stealing stuff. Any moment now, he'll come in here. I need to think quickly. The bathroom is nearly empty, and the only dangerous thing I have is my shaving razer, and that's not going to do anything against someone bigger and stronger than me.

I swallow, fear coursing through my veins, as I look around the bathroom. And then I get an idea. Since boxes of Jace's clothes are in front of the towel rack, I never hung my towel on it. Instead, I'd thrown a new towel over the wall of the shower. Slowly, I take the towel, my heart thudding like crazy. I know it's not the greatest plan, but it's the only one I have.

Whoever is in my room will eventually walk in here. And then I'll throw this towel around their neck and pull it as tightly as I can. Oh god. Just the thought of it sends a terrifying wave of nausea through me. I can't handle this? What am I supposed to do?

I curse myself for leaving my cell phone in the other room. The shadow moves in front of the door. My heart beats so hard I can hear it in my skull. The shadow says something. His voice is deep, but just a vibration that I can't make out from the sound of the water and my beating heart.

I grip the towel in my hand. Standing in the shower, I am hidden by the steam on the glass. The shadow moves closer, says something else.

"Can you hear me?"

And then I let out the breath I'd been holding. Relief sweeps over me like a hurricane, I lean forward and wipe away the steam from the glass. Jace stares at me from the other side of the shower, a crooked smile on his face.

I turn off the water and open the door. "You scared the hell out of me!" I say. My voice shakes, and I look down at the towel clenched in my hands, realizing that I'm shaking and it's not from being cold.

"Aww," Jace says, laughing. "I'm sorry, Bay. I didn't mean to scare you. I was talking the whole time but you never answered so I guess you couldn't hear me."

"Ya think?" I say, trying to laugh, but I'm still recovering from the fright of a freaking lifetime. I take a deep breath and toss the towel back over the glass wall.

Jace wiggles his eyebrows. "You're sexy as hell," he says, his eyes raking over my naked, shivering body.

I roll my eyes and turn the hot water back on. "I'm mad at you," I say, turning around. "You don't get to see the goods when I'm mad at you."

He lets out a low whistle. "Babe you just turned around, and that view is even better."

My face flushes and I slam the door closed, but this time I can't help but laugh. "Go away!" I say. "Aren't you supposed to be getting pizza?"

The music shuts off from the computer and Jace walks back into the bathroom. He leans against the glass, cupping his hands around his eyes to try to get a peek inside the shower. "We decided that Mommy should come with us and get food that she wants to eat, so we came home to pick you up."

I sigh, shaking my head even though he can't see it. He'd done something nice for me and nearly scared me to death in the process.

"So what do you say?" Jace calls out. "Mexican food, maybe?"

"Sounds good," I say, closing my eyes and letting the water run down my body. "Give me five minutes."

CHAPTER 2

I don't know what time it is when I wake up the next morning, but I refuse to open my eyes. It's Sunday, our off day, and the sunlight has already filtered in through the windows so I know it's not ridiculously early. But probably still early. I don't care. I roll over and put my arm over my eyes, wanting to stay asleep as long as the baby monitor on my nightstand will let me.

I drift off for a few minutes and then stir again when Jace nudges my arm. "You awake?" he says in a half-whisper.

I squeeze my eyes shut. "No."

"Sounds like you are," he says, leaning down and kissing my neck. I squirm from the tickle but keep my eyes closed. He nudges me again. "I'm bored . . . wake up."

I shake my head. "Nope. Not till the baby makes me."

"I used you be your baby," he says, nudging me relentlessly on the shoulder. "Then the real baby was born and I got shoved aside."

I roll my eyes and turn around to face him.

"Ha! It worked!" he says, wrapping his arms around me and pulling me close. I tuck into his chest, letting his arms warm me up.

"I don't want to wake up yet," I say, snuggling against his shoulder.

He runs his fingers through my hair. "I'm not used to being in bed this late. I know I should be happy but it just feels weird."

I close my eyes and inhale his earthy scent. I love the feeling of his arms around me. "You work way too hard babe," I murmur, my lips just an inch away from his bare chest. "You should take more days off."

"I will, once the business is more established." He chuckles. "I mean, I hope I do. For now, I'll just enjoy this day with you and the kid."

"I'm surprised he's still asleep," I say, feeling

sleep tug at me once again. "It has to be like seven a.m. or so."

"He'll be out a little longer," Jace says, all matter-of-factly.

"What makes you think that?" I ask.

"He woke up at five and I ran around the house with him for two hours. He got so tired he passed back out."

I wrap my arm around his chest and pull him a little bit closer to me. "You're the best."

He snorts. "Duh."

WHEN WE'RE ALL UP AND ENJOYING OUR SUNDAY OFF work, I order Chinese food takeout for lunch. Jace and Jett play a game on the Xbox—well, Jace plays while sitting on the floor in front of the TV. Jett sits in his lap, playing with another controller that doesn't have any batteries in it. He laughs and squeals every time Jace crashes the car on the screen. I lounge on the couch, drinking tea and watching the cuteness as it unfolds.

Sure, Jace is hot as hell when he's shirtless, bent over his dirt bike, tools spread out around him while he's trying to fix something that's broken. But he's even hotter when he's doing little things like playing a video game with our kid. He makes such a great dad. It's like he doesn't even have to try.

The television screen erupts into an explosion as Jace crashes two cars together and Jett shrieks with joy. I smile, and then a stab of pain hits me as I think about my own mom. She had to raise me and my brother without the aid of our dad being in the picture. She never got these sweet moments in the living room on a lazy Sunday. She never got lazy Sundays.

I stare into my tea cup and remind myself of all of the things that make my life wonderful. I have so much to be grateful for, and sometimes it feels like I didn't do anything to deserve it. Actually, *all* of the time it feels like I don't deserve it.

"You okay babe?" Jace calls out over his shoulder. His eyes don't leave the TV.

"Huh?" I say. "Yeah, I'm fine."

"You just sighed." He pauses the game and looks back at me. "It sounded like one of those sighs where you're mad at me."

I roll my eyes. "You're a dork. And I'm not mad at you. I'm just . . . thinking."

"Uh oh," Jace says, making big eyes at Jett who stares up at him from his lap. "Mommy's thinking.

We should probably run away."

Jett grins and bashes his game controller, looking back at the TV as if he expects something to happen to it. "We can turn the game off," Jace says, looking to me for an answer. "Do you want to watch TV or something?"

"No, honey," I say, stretching out my legs across the couch. "I am perfectly happy with how things are. I was just sighing because life is so perfect."

His eyes narrow and he waits a beat, probably verifying that I really mean it. "I'm serious!" I say, sticking out my tongue.

"Cool," he says, seemingly satisfied with my answer. "Because all I want to do is sit on my ass all day and enjoy this day off."

"We really should unpack some boxes," I say, looking around.

"Sorry babe, I can't hear you," Jace says sarcastically.

I laugh. And then his phone rings from the couch pillow beside me. I lean over and look at the screen. "It's Park."

"Can you answer it?" Jace says, still playing the video game.

"Hello?" I say cheerfully into Jace's phone.

"Damn, man, you sound girly in the mornings," Park says. I can hear the smile in his voice.

"Oh *ha* ha," I say. "Why are you calling on Jace's day off? Is my best friend not keeping you entertained?"

"I wish I was calling because I'm bored," he says. "We kind of have an issue over here."

"Oh no."

Jace looks back at me, concern stitched on his brow. "Is this the kind of issue that needs Jace?" I ask Park.

"Yeah, unfortunately. It's nothing to worry about, just some bullshit with the contracts."

"You want to talk to him?"

"Nah, just tell him to put some clothes on and get over here."

I lift an eyebrow. "What makes you think he's naked?"

He chuckles. "He's home with you. I mean duh."

I laugh and Jace gives me a weird look from his place on the floor. "See ya later, Park."

Jace pauses the game and smooths Jett's messy blonde hair down. "Am I going into work?" he asks, making an exaggerated puppy frown.

I make the same frown. "Yep."

After kissing Jace goodbye, I get a marvelous idea. I call up Becca and ask if she's bored.

"Of course I'm bored," she says with a groan. "Park and I were supposed to hang out all day and then he got stuck working."

"That's why you have me," I say, grinning mischievously. "I was thinking since we're both stuck with nothing to do, that maybe you should come over here and help me unpack."

"You know what, that doesn't even seem too bad," she says. "I'll be there in five."

TOGETHER, BECCA AND I MANAGE TO UNPACK THE entire kitchen. We play pretend cooking like weirdos to find which cabinets would be the best to store certain types of kitchen utensils. Jett has a blast playing with the boxes after we've emptied them and soon we've moved into the living room and then the study. We hang photos and décor on the walls, string curtains over the curtain rods. I stack books on the bookshelf and Becca organizes the coats in the hall closet.

Things move so quickly with her help that I start to regret not doing this sooner. The house is already so gorgeous and new and shiny and now with our stuff unpacked from the ugly boxes, it looks even better.

"You kept your maternity clothes?" Becca asks once we've migrated into my bedroom. She's been unpacking clothes and hanging them up in the closet, while I tackle boxes of shoes that are all out of order.

I shrug. "Yeah, they were expensive. Which is funny because most of the time I just wore leggings and Jace's baggy t-shirts."

She wiggles her eyebrows at me as she slips a hanger into a pink flowy maternity shirt. "You planning on having baby number two soon?"

"Who the hell said anything about another baby?" I ask, jerking backward as if the thought alone was scary.

She laughs. "Come on! Jett needs a brother or sister. Don't you, Jett?" She coos at my two-year-old, who grins up at her. He's been playing with one of his daddy's dirt bike trophies which had somehow ended up in a box of clothes.

I know she's just messing with me, but I take a moment to think about the question seriously. I mean, Jett was a total accident. I was still a teenager and hadn't planned on having a kid anytime soon.

And although everything has worked out incredibly well, I would still never recommend having a kid at such a young age to anyone. And although I think it's cool to have all of your kids kind of close in age so that they grow up together—I don't know if I should do the same thing since we're still so young.

I shrug. "I don't know."

"Oh, come on. Surely you want another kiddo."

I glance over at the kiddo I already have and smile. He is such a great kid and I love him more than I love anything on this planet. But I also remember the pain of childbirth, the late nights and lack of sleep. Cleaning up baby puke and making bottles at four in the morning. Changing diapers and cleaning off snotty noses.

"I really don't know," I say honestly. Then I give her a coy smile. "Why, are you planning on starting a family with Park?"

She snorts and waves her hand at my question. "Not anytime soon." She holds up her left hand. "I need a rock on this finger first."

I nod. "I'm sure you'll get one any day now."

CHAPTER 3

Monday is ridiculously busy at the Track, but we manage to keep up with all of the work pretty well. The only thing that bothers me is trying to run the front desk and keep up with Jace at the same time. I refuse to let him out of my sight, and that makes it difficult to deal with clients and answering phones and running back and forth throughout the building. And several times a day I have to walk across the track to get Jace or Park when they're training someone and don't have their phones on them. Carrying a two-year-old makes all of that difficult.

In the evening, Jace grills burgers for us on the grill. We're hanging out on the back patio of our new home, using the new grill he bought the day after we moved in. Jace is a great cook and an even better griller. I chop up a hamburger patty into small pieces for Jett and slide the plate over to him in his high chair.

"Hey, babe?" I ask, admiring Jace's sculpted arms while he works the grill. "I need to run an idea past you."

"Do you want me to go upstairs and strip naked because, if so, yes I'll do that."

I roll my eyes at his cocky grin. "Maybe later, but this is serious."

He takes a plate and makes himself a burger then sits in the patio chair next to me. "What's up?"

Part of me is embarrassed for even asking but the other part of me thinks it's a good idea. I take a deep breath and lay out my plan, just as I'd rehearsed in my head. "Okay, so I don't know how much influence I have over business decisions since you're technically the owner and all," I begin.

Jace's brows draw together and he talks with his mouth full of food. "You have a ton of influence," he says, swallowing. "It's your business too, babe."

"Well . . . so I was thinking that we should hire someone."

"For what kind of job?" he asks.

"Like, a babysitter. I don't know," I say, shaking

my head. "I'm going crazy keeping up with Jett while I'm doing my own job, and I don't want to take him to a daycare. Besides, all of the daycares around here are so far away I'd take me a lot longer to get to work if I had to drop him off each day. And they're so expensive I was thinking we could hire another person to help watch him and also help us out, and—I don't know," I say with a shrug. "Maybe it's a dumb idea."

"No, I like it. I mean, that's why we built the kid's room after all. So people would have a place for their little kids so they wouldn't be hot outside or running around outside in danger of being hit by a dirt bike." Jace nods, his eyes looking far off as he thinks it over. "Do you have anyone in mind?"

I shrug. "No, but I was thinking we could advertise it on the Track's Facebook page and stuff. Just put out a hiring add and see who applies."

"Cool," he says, puffing out his cheeks to make a goofy face at Jett. "Let's do it."

I smile and it's like a ton of weight has just lifted off my shoulders. Now I just need to find someone I'd trust around my kid.

After dinner, Jace puts Jett to bed, which turns out to be ridiculously easy because he was so worn out from playing all day. But when Jace brags about how great of a dad he is because he had Jett to sleep in a few minutes, I go ahead and let him gloat.

I take a hot shower, knowing that although I'm relaxed now, tomorrow is another day of hectic work and running around after my kid all day. At least tomorrow I'll get to post a job opening online and maybe find my dream babysitter-slash-employee.

I'm walking out of the bathroom, toweling off my hair when I see Jace. He's sitting on the foot of our bed, wearing only his boxers. His hands rest on his thighs and he peers at me, a smirk on his lips. He's gained about ten pounds of muscle in the last few months, from working out at our new gym every day. He has a slight tan line on his bicep from wearing t-shirts while training clients all day in the sun.

I walk slowly toward him, wearing only a t-shirt I stole from his side of the closet. "Hey there, handsome."

He wiggles his fingers, signaling for me to walk closer to him. "I missed you," he says, his voice throaty as I approach him at the end of the bed.

"I was only gone for fifteen minutes," I say, putting a hand on my hip.

"Fifteen minutes is a long time," he says. He

grabs my waist in his hands, tugging me forward until I fall into his lap. I lift my legs and straddle him, wrapping my arms around his shoulders.

"How are you always so happy to see me?" I tease as I run my fingers through his hair. "You see me every night and every night you're happy about it."

"Why wouldn't I be?" he says, dipping his hands down to my bare thighs and sliding his fingers up under my shirt. Goosebumps prickle across my skin at the feel of his calloused hands sliding up my waist. He leans forward and gives me a quick kiss. "You're my favorite person."

I try to reply but my breath catches in my throat when his lips press a kiss to my neck. His hands slide up, over my ribs, his thumbs caressing my breasts as he lifts the shirt up and over my head. He tosses it to the floor.

I close my eyes and lean forward, expecting a make out session. Instead, he holds me by my shoulders, and smiles. I open my eyes. "What are you doing?"

He shrugs. "Just checking you out. You're insanely hot, you know."

I've also been hitting the gym every day since we opened the business and I know it shows. My arms are toned, my waist is smaller than it's ever been and my legs are well-defined. Although I'm really proud of myself, it's also a little weird to be in such great shape. I've never worked out before. I roll my eyes. "I'm not that hot."

He shakes his head, then teases my collarbone with a flick of his tongue. "You're crazy hot. And kind of a badass now. I wouldn't pick a fight with you."

"That's because you're my husband and you respect me more than that," I say.

He shakes his head. "It's because I'm afraid you'd kick my ass." He laughs and leans backward, pulling me on top of him. "And I'd probably love every second of it."

I throw a playful punch to his chest and he smirks. "Yeah baby, just like that."

I can't help but laugh at him. "You once told me that you'd love me no matter what I looked like and now you clearly love me more now that I'm hotter."

He shakes his head and lets his hands roam my body. "Not true. I'll still love you no matter what. I'm just saying—your new body has attracted a lot of attention around the track."

This makes me pause. "Huh?"

He shakes his head. "It's nothing. I've just had

to hear quite a few comments on how hot you are from guys who don't know you're my wife. It's hard not to punch a client in the face, ya know?"

"Interesting," I say, leaning in to kiss him again.

"That's enough talking," Jace whispers with his lips to mine. Then he pulls me closer and shows me exactly how much he loves me.

I STARE AT MY POST ON THE TRACK'S FACEBOOK page.

WE'RE HIRING AT THE TRACK! SEEKING SOMEONE energetic and good with kids to work in our kid's room. Duties are primarily childcare for a two-year-old, but may be required to watch other children for clients from time to time. Must be responsible! Fans of motocross a plus.

I READ OVER IT YET AGAIN, WONDERING IF IT'LL attract any attention. I've never been in charge of this kind of thing before, so I'm just making it up as I go along. Jace has already had a few of his clients say they have a teenaged daughter who might be interested, but so far we don't have any official applications. Of course, the ad has only been up for an hour.

When Becca comes over to take my place at the front counter so I can get a lunch break, I decide to sneak into the gym for a short workout. I've spent the whole day just sitting behind the front desk answering phones and talking to people and I am dying to stretch out my muscles and move around.

Plus, I'm kind of still thinking about the comment Jace made last night about people thinking I'm hot. It's the most flattering and weird thing that's ever happened to me. I want to be attractive for my own personal reasons—mainly to make Jace proud and have him drooling over me like he did last night. But as far as working out goes, I've been doing this for myself. I'm stronger and I feel amazing and I never need to ask Jace to open jars of grape jelly anymore. All of these are good reasons to work out. I don't exactly try to look hot for anyone but Jace.

But knowing people think I am hot . . . well, that's cool.

"There she is," Park says, walking into the gym. "Hey, Bayleigh, do you have a second?"

I'm sitting in a weight machine, doing shoulder

presses and although I can hear him, I can't see him without letting go of the bars.

"What's up?" I ask between reps. Then I hear two sets of footsteps. I let go and turn around. Park walks up to me and a guy I've never seen before is trailing him. He's probably in his thirties and he's some kind of bodybuilder, based on his huge chest. His arms are covered in tattoos and he wears a thick silver chain around his neck.

"I have someone looking for you," Park explains, gesturing to the guy.

"Hi," I say, standing up and extending my hand. "Are you looking to sign up for the gym?"

"Not exactly," he says in a deep voice. He hands me a business card. "My name is Mark Brooks, owner of Texas Motocross Magazine. Do you have a second?"

"Sure." I smile. "I mean, I wish I wasn't covered in sweat," I say with a chuckle. "But I'm free to talk. What's up?"

Park gets my attention. "You good? I'm gonna head back outside."

I nod and he excuses himself.

"So what can I do for you, Mark?" I ask, grabbing my sweat towel off the rack and swiping it over my face.

"I was wondering if you'd be interested in working with me for next month's magazine issue," Mark begins. He takes out his cell phone and holds it out so we can both see it. He's on his own magazine's Facebook page.

"Oh, sure. Like an article on the Track?" I ask.

"Sort of, but not exactly." His eyes meet mine. "Have you ever done any modeling?"

"Uh . . ." I laugh because it's awkward. "No."

He smiles. "Well, I want to show you something," he says, scrolling for something on his phone. "I'm a motocross racer as well as a personal trainer. My magazine covers Texas motocross races and tracks, but it also has a lot of bodybuilder readers as well. We place a huge emphasis on fitness in our magazine, since, as I'm sure you know, it takes a lot of endurance to race a dirt bike."

I nod. "You should probably talk to Jace about this though. I don't ride, I just help run the business."

"Nope, you're who we want. See, we're trying to include more women in our magazine. Two weeks ago, someone posted a photo to our Facebook page and people loved it." He holds out his phone to me and my jaw drops. The picture is of me and Jace and I had no idea anyone snapped a photo of this moment. I take the guy's phone right from his hand and hold it closer to my face, just to get a good look.

I remember this day, not too long ago. It was after hours and I had been working out in the gym. A few of our clients were working out as well. I was lying on my back on the incline press. Jace was spotting me, standing behind the bench. At one point, in between lifting the weight bar, Jace had bent forward and kissed me, in a cute upside-down kiss. This person snapped a photo at that moment.

"That's really cute," I say, handing the phone back to him.

"Did you see the comments?" he asks.

I shake my head. Truthfully, I'd been admiring Jace's biceps in the photo and hadn't noticed anything else. Mark scrolls down quickly and I can see there's probably a hundred comments on the photo. My heart leaps into my throat. "What do they say?"

"Everyone loved it. Jace is already a fan favorite with our magazine readers, but the women really resonated about the idea of a wife working out with her husband. If you're up for it, we'd like to do an article about The Track, from your point of view. Talk about a day in the life of Bayleigh Adams, working at the business, working out with Jace, all of it."

He slides the phone back into his pocket and gives me an eager smile. "So what do you think?"

"Why did you mention modeling?" I ask as a swarm of emotions flow through me at once.

"We'd have a professional photographer come out and get some photos to use for the article," he explains. "We'd want you to pose for them of course. We can have Jace in it as well, but this would mainly be a piece about you."

All of the air rushes out of my lungs. I never set out to become famous in my life, but, an article based on me? The wife of the guy everyone loves? My lips twist into a smile. "How could I say no to that, Mark?"

He smiles and shakes my hand. "I look forward to working with you."

CHAPTER 4

I find Jace as soon as he's finished with his client and I'm so excited I can't stop bouncing on my toes. We're standing outside near the bleachers and he watches me with a weird fascination.

"What is it?" he asks, grabbing my arms to steady me.

I stop bouncing and grin up at him. "Do you know the guy who runs Texas Motocross Magazine?"

Jace nods. "Mark, right?"

My grin widens. I grab Jace's shoulders and tell him all about my impromptu meeting with Mark and about the article and the photoshoot. Partway through I start getting nervous that maybe he'll have some kind of problem with it, like maybe he doesn't want me doing an article about our lives.

But as soon as I finish telling him the story, he is all smiles.

"Babe!" he says, pulling me in for a quick kiss. "That is awesome!"

"I know, right?" I have to bite the inside of my lip to keep from smiling like an idiot. "Oh, and you have to look up that picture on his Facebook page. It is so cute."

"Will do," he says, kissing me again. "I have a client arriving soon so we'll talk more later, okay?"

"Okay," I say, squeezing his hand. As I walk back to the building, I am filled with a sense of accomplishment, even though I didn't really do much to earn it. Still, someone out there thinks my life as Jace's wife, Jett's mom, and a business manager is worth writing about. And that's pretty cool.

I tell myself not to let it get to my head, because it's not like I'm suddenly famous or anything. But still, it is pretty awesome. When I get back inside, I tell Becca the whole story again and she's just as psyched as Jace was. We spend five minutes giggling and freaking out about it, and even Jett seems excited too, although he has no idea what we're talking about.

"Oh, by the way," Becca says, reaching for a stack of papers behind the front counter. "These are for you."

"What are they?" I ask, wrinkling my eyebrows. "Wait . . ." I flip through the stack. There's at least ten papers, all different and some of them printed on colorful paper. "Are these resumes?"

Becca nods. "Yep. Apparently some people thought they'd be more likely to get the job if they applied in person instead of online. They were all pretty disappointed when I told them I didn't know where you were. One girl said she'd be back in an hour."

"Cool," I say with a nod. "This is weird. I'm like, still trying to figure out how to interview people," I say with a laugh. "I don't think I'm prepared to talk to someone right now!"

Becca nods. "Yeah, it is weird. It's like we're too young to be hiring people, ya know?"

"Exactly," I say.

Becca shrugs and claps me on the shoulder. "Good thing this is your problem and not mine," she says with a snort.

I groan. "Why are you my best friend again?" I ask teasingly.

She blows me a kiss. "Because I'm awesome."

MY PHOTOSHOOT IS SCHEDULED FOR NEXT WEEK, SO I hit the gym extra hard each day in order to look as amazing as possible for it. The résumés from potential child care employees are pouring in and by the third day, Becca and I have a huge stack to go through. We narrow them down by removing the résumés of clearly crazy people, aka-a guy who listed dealing stolen prescription pills as his previous job experience, and focusing on people with good qualities.

"What about this one?" I ask, holding up a pale pink piece of paper.

Becca's eyebrow quirks. "You're only picking it because it's pink."

I laugh. "That's why I looked at it, but still . . . She looks very qualified." I hold up the paper. "She's seventeen and she's worked at her mom's daycare since she was fourteen. She says she also grew up there with her mom so she knows all the ins and outs of childcare and she's CPR certified.

She doesn't live far away." I look at Becca and press the pink paper to my chest. "I want to hire this girl."

"Gimme," she says, taking the paper to read over it herself. "Damn, this is impressive," she says a moment later. "Her name is Deja Williams. Call her now," she says, rattling off the phone number.

A trill of anxiety and excitement flows through me at the idea of interviewing our first employee. And not just any employee—one that will help me directly with my job. I dial her number and Becca and I make big-eyed excited grins at each other as I wait for Deja to answer. She answers on the second ring and sounds just as perfect as I'd expected her to on the phone. She agrees to come in for an interview in the morning. When we hang up, Becca and I squee.

"Should we call other people for interviews, too?" she asks, shuffling the other résumés.

I bite my lip. "Let's see how it goes with Deja first. I mean, she's pretty much already got the job in my mind."

"You are a very determined person," she says, walking over to the work computer at the end of the counter. She pulls up the Track's Facebook page and types something.

"What are you doing?" I ask, shoving in beside her.

She grins. "Nothing. Just complaining about how weird the boss's wife is . . ."

My eyes go wide but then I see that she's only posting about the upcoming gym membership special that Park came up with earlier today. I shove her in the arm. "I don't know why I keep falling for your jokes," I mutter as I look back at Deja's resume.

"Um, Bay?" Becca says a minute later. "You might want to see this."

Jace walks in the front door at the same time, his expression hard to read. He's definitely not mad, but maybe he's a little amused? "Have you see the —" he begins, only to stop when he sees the computer screen. "Yep, you have."

"Seen what?" I ask, moving over to look at the Facebook page.

Becca scrolls up and I read what our Facebook followers have been saying. Earlier today, Mark made a post on his magazine's page and he tagged The Track in it. It talks about how their new issue will include a feature of me. And then I read the comments.

. . .

JACE'S WIFE IS SO FREAKING HOT.

WHY DO CHICKS ALWAYS FALL FOR THE FAST GUYS? Can't a slow ass rider like me ever get one, lol.

THAT'S JACE ADAM'S WIFE? SHIT, I SHOULD probably stop hitting on her every time I see her.

WOOHOO! FINALLY SOME GIRLS IN YOUR MAGAZINE that aren't vapid models.

THAT LAST COMMENT WAS FROM A LADY THAT LOOKS old enough to be someone's grandmother. My lips slide to the side of my mouth. "This is weird," I say, not knowing what to make of the comments. I mean I guess I should be flattered? But this is so weird.

Jace slides an arm around my waist and tugs me to him in a side hug. "My wife is more famous than I am. I'm a little jealous."

I roll my eyes. "Whatever. I'm not anywhere close to your famousness. Besides," I say, rising up on my toes to kiss him, "I've had to put up with your famousness for three years. It's time for you to get some of your own medicine."

His hand slides lower and he squeezes my ass. "I'm man enough to handle it," he says with a wink. He points to the computer screen. "But if that guy comes in here and hits on you again I'm going to whoop his ass."

CHAPTER 5

Jace looks up from his fast food breakfast sandwich when I walk into work the next morning. He smiles and shakes his head at me.

"What?" I say, bending down to let Jett slip off my hip so he can run to his daddy.

"You are ridiculously excited about this job interview, huh?" he says, taking a sip of coffee. "You're practically bouncing off the walls. I take it she'll be here soon?"

"Yes and don't make fun of me for being excited," I say, sticking out my tongue. I walk over to him and slip my arms around his back, watching him while he eats and goes over his client list at the same time.

"I'm still thinking about last night," he says, his voice low. I look up at him, still clinging tightly to him.

"Oh yeah?" I say, leaning against his arm. "Tell me more."

"I loooove when you're on top," he whispers. There's no one else in the room but our two-year-old, but his low voice sends a rush of desire through me. "It's sexy as hell."

"Well maybe you'll get that again tonight," I say, smiling.

He wiggles his eyebrows and turns around, slipping his hands around my waist. I slide my hands up his chest and wrap them around his neck. "I love you," he says.

"I love *you*," I say, smiling as I pull up to kiss him. He tastes like coffee.

"Daddy!" Jett squeals. We both look down and find him banging on Jace's leg with his little chubby fist. "Daddy, pick," he says, wanting to be picked up.

Jace levels a seductive gaze at me. "We'll finish this talk later?"

I nod once. "Meet me in our special meeting place, tonight at nine."

"Cool," he says, bending to pick up Jett. "Wait, we have a meeting place?"

I put a hand on my hip. "I meant our bed. Obviously."

"Ah," he says and I swear a see a hint of pink fill his tanned cheeks. "I'll be there."

DEJA ARRIVES EXACTLY ON TIME. NOT THAT I HAD expected anything less from the job applicant I've already hired in my mind. She's short, sweet, and very pretty with brown skin and dark hair that's pulled back in a perky ponytail. She calls me Mrs. Adams and she's polite and perfect and everything I could want in a person who will help me care for Jett.

"So, your main job would be watching Jett, my two-year-old," I say, after we've started talking more about the job and less about her. "I'm kind of the business manager around here so I'm always running around doing whatever needs to be done and I just need to know that Jett is safe so I don't have to worry about him."

"I'm really great with kids," she says, smiling. "So that shouldn't be a problem."

I lean forward. "Would you like to meet Jett?"

She beams. "Totally!"

My final test for hiring her is to see how she gets along with Jett. And the meeting goes better than I could have planned. I show her the kid's room and she's clearly impressed with it, which makes me feel awesome about my decorating skills. And then after a while, Becca, who had been playing with Jett while I conducted the interview, leaves us with him and heads back to man the front desk.

Jett takes to her immediately, smiling and laughing as she drops to the floor to play with him. When she tells me he's the cutest kid she's ever seen, I am totally enamored with her.

I sit on the couch next to where Deja plays with Jett and his toy train. "So, Deja," I say, clasping my hands together. "I'd love to offer you the job, if you're still interested?"

She beams. "Oh my god, really? I would love to work here. This place is awesome and Jett is *so* cute."

I grin, feeling a little guilty about the stack of applicants that I never bothered to bring in for an interview. But this isn't about spending forever trying to hire someone—when it comes to my son, it's a gut feeling. And Deja and Jett are a perfect match. They're already friends and he's only known her a short while.

"So, when can you start?"

CHAPTER 6

The Track is packed full of people on the day my magazine interview and photoshoot is supposed to take place. It's a beautiful January morning, and much warmer than usual for this time of year, so I guess that's why everyone wanted to come out today.

Jace and Park are fully booked with training clients for the entire day, from five in the morning until eight at night. There's even walk-in clients who knew they couldn't get an appointment but begged to just hang out and watch Jace and Park teach others. And hiring Deja couldn't have come at a better time because now there's three other kids in the kid room with her and Jett. She assures me she can handle it all though, so I apologize for the thousandth time and head into the main office when it's time for my interview.

I'm expecting Mark again, but a tall lanky guy with a computer bag slung over his shoulder smiles at me as I enter the room. "Mrs. Adams?" he asks, extending a hand to me. "I'm Ricky."

"Hi Ricky," I say, donning a polite smile. "Are you with Mark?"

"I'm here instead of Mark," he explains. "I'm the writer so I'll be writing your article myself."

"Ah okay, cool," I say, suddenly a little bit nervous. From now on, everything he sees me do could possibly go in the article about me. So I need to be on my best behavior.

I lead him into Jace's office, which is the only quiet area of the building so that we can talk. He tells me that the photographer will be here in a little bit and that all of the photoshoot stuff will be up to that guy.

Becca brings us coffee, which was totally on her because I didn't even think of that, and Ricky looks impressed at the gesture. "Call me if you need anything, Mrs. Adams," Becca says, smiling in this way that only I, as her best friend, would understand. She's pretending to be some kind of perfect assistant in order to make me look even more professional and awesome in front of this writer. I keep my composure, but inside I'm grinning like a dork. This is fun.

Ricky takes out a notebook and a handheld recorder. "Do you mind if I record this?" he asks, but something tells me I don't really have a choice.

"Not at all," I say, mentally telling myself not to say anything stupid.

"Great," he says, placing the recorder on Jace's desk right between us. "So, Mrs. Adams, let's begin."

"You can just call me Bayleigh," I say. Although I'm almost twenty-one and it's fun to have Jace's last name, sometimes being called Mrs. Adams just makes me feel old. Like a teacher, or the old lady who lives next door or something.

Ricky nods and marks something on this notebook. "So, Bayleigh, you're married to a former professional motocross racer who is now the owner of an incredibly successful company. How much pressure do you feel to maintain your trophy wife status?"

I'm silent for a minute. Surely he's just joking right? When he lifts his eyebrows, anxiously awaiting a reply, I laugh. "Um, I'm not a trophy wife," I say. "So I guess to answer your question, I don't feel any pressure? Because I'm not a trophy wife."

"Hmm," he says, scribbling on his notebook. "What makes you say that? You're a beautiful young woman who is married to a professional racer—"

"He's not a professional racer anymore," I say, interrupting him. "He hasn't been since the day I met him. We fell in love as normal people, not as a famous guy who was looking for a trophy." Now that I'm talking, I find it impossible to stop. I need this nerdy writer guy to understand that I'm not some stupid girl trying to be famous on the arm of her famous husband. "He chose a boring life with me over pursuing fame again, and that's really all there is to it. Our marriage wasn't part of a master plan."

"Well said," Ricky says, writing something in his notebook again. He smiles and it seems like he has a new kind of respect for me. I guess maybe he was expecting me to play the part of "dumb trophy wife" or something. I sit a little straighter.

"Okay next question," he says, leaning back in his chair. "Tell me about the daily life of a woman running a business with her husband."

AFTER WHAT STARTED OUT AS A WEIRD INTERVIEW, my talk with Ricky wasn't all that bad. He never brought up the whole teen pregnancy thing and I was grateful for that. When we're done, I'm confident that his article can't say anything too bad or scandalous about my life, and that's a good thing.

The photographer arrives and this time Mark is with him. I check on Jett, who is happy and playing with Deja, and then we head into the gym for the photoshoot. Mark's photographer is almost a clone of him, all muscular and beefy and fake-tanned. His name is Ace and he looks like he belongs in a motorcycle club instead of behind the lens of an expensive camera. They also have a fashion expert with them, a pixie of a woman with bright pink hair and a ton of eyeshadow.

She makes me wear a pair of extra short cutoff jeans. The kind that are so short, the bottoms of the pockets hang out the front. Then I wear a bright pink tank top that she pulls up and ties in a knot in the back. I'm really glad I've been working on my abs because they're on full display.

I'm photographed straddling one of Jace's dirt bikes, sitting on weight benches, and sitting on top of the front counter. They wouldn't let me just stand behind it, I had to be on top. The whole thing is provocative and sexy and I'm not sure if it's cool or kind of terrifying. I'm not exactly the type to pose all sexy for a magazine. I mean, sure I've gotten in shape lately and I'm proud of my body. But, that doesn't stop me from feeling silly as I pose with my cleavage on full display.

Jace is so busy all day, he never has time to stop by while the photographer is here and I'm kind of grateful for it. I'm not sure what he'd say about the whole thing. But eventually it's over, and Mark and his crew go home, promising to email me some of their favorite photos later on.

Deja, Becca, and I take Jett out to dinner once we close the front office for the day. They want to know all about my experience with the interview and photo shoot and we gossip about it until nine at night when Jace calls me.

"Hey babe," I say, answering the phone.

"Have you checked the track's email account?" he says, his voice sounding a little amused.

"No, why?" I say with a sigh. "What drama has happened this time?"

"Not a work emergency," he says. I can hear clicking in the background. "I just wrapped up a client and came inside to check some emails and damn, my wife is hot."

"Huh?" I ask. Jett starts to whine and Deja distracts him by making a goofy face. "Wait, did Mark email you?"

"Yup," Jace says with a little laugh. "These pictures are smoking."

I groan. "I don't want to see them. I'm too scared."

"No reason to be scared, babe. Let me put it this way—I am really excited for our bedroom meeting tonight."

I blush at the sultry tone of his voice and turn to the side in our restaurant booth, hoping the girls can't see me. "Is that so?"

"Mmhmm," he says. "Although I'm not sure I want the entire Texas motocross scene seeing how freaking hot my wife is. The thought alone kind of makes me want to punch something."

I snort. "Whatever. I won't be anything compared to the other girls they put in that magazine."

"No you won't," he says. "You're way hotter."

I roll my eyes and try to play it off but a part of me feels bad. Jace is being a really good sport about this whole thing but I can tell there's a hint of jealousy in his voice. How would I feel if he took sexy shirtless photos to put in a magazine? The thought alone makes a knot form in my stomach.

Suddenly this entire whirlwind of a day comes crashing down on me. Maybe this wasn't such a good idea, after all.

CHAPTER 7

Gasping for breath, I roll off of Jace and bury my head in a pillow. "That was epic," I say, panting.

"Um, hell yeah it was," Jace says, sliding a hand over my bare skin. Chills tingle at his touch and he rolls over, cuddling me in our bed. "You've been like a crazy sex princess ever since that magazine guy talked to you. Not that I'm complaining. It's amazing."

"Crazy sex princess?" I say, turning so my face is no longer smashed into the pillow. "That sounds like a band name. And yeah, the photoshoot might have done something for my confidence."

It's been a week since the photo shoot and the magazine article should be coming out soon. I've felt like a total badass every day since then and I can't wait to see the article. I'll probably frame it and hang it on the wall . . . in every single room. Ha!

Jace nuzzles his scruffy face into my neck and we cuddle up, with me as the little spoon. He slides his hand down my arm and links his fingers in between mine. We're both naked and a little sweaty, but I don't mind it. We stay like this for a while, cuddled in each other's arms, enjoying just being together. It's one of those rare moments lately where we actually have time to spend with each other.

I roll over and look at the clock. "It's only ten-thirty," I say, realizing that our epic love making session didn't take more than forty-five minutes after we put Jett to sleep in his room. "We still have time to watch TV or something."

Jace runs his tongue along my neck. "Or we could forget the television and do it again."

His voice is raspy and like honey all at the same time. I smile and squirm under the kisses he places in the most ticklish spots on my collarbone. "I could do that," I say, turning onto my back. He props his head up on his elbow and traces circles on my stomach with his other hand.

"I love you, Bay," he says as his eyes meet mine. The windows are dark and the only light comes from the soft glow of a lamp in the corner of the room. It makes him look sexy and dangerous as he hovers over me, his hand reaching up to cup my cheek.

"I love you," I say, kissing him.

He pulls my bottom lip in between his teeth and then slips his tongue into my mouth. I grab for him and pull him on top of me, sliding my hands around his muscled back. We kiss for a long time, our lips caressing each other until I can't stand it any longer. I whimper and Jace chuckles to himself.

"Sorry, I like teasing you."

"You're so mean," I say, frowning.

He kisses the frown right off of my lips.

"I have an idea," I whisper, as he grinds against me.

"And what is that?" he says, his voice hitching as I dig my nails into his back.

"We should do a photoshoot together next time. Like a husband and wife thing."

He glances at me and then lowers his head, kissing my neck while his hand slides across my breast. "That'd be fun," he whispers, his breath tickling my skin. "Of course no one would be looking at me if they printed photos of the both of us."

"Yeah right," I say, gasping as he presses into me. "A ton of girls would like to get a good look at these abs." I run my fingers down his chest and he draws in a sharp breath.

"That's enough talking," he says, his voice nearly a growl. "I'm going crazy just lying here. I need you."

I grin and wrap my arms around his neck, pulling him close to me. My legs part and wrap around him and he loves me the way he is so very good at.

Later, when Jace has fallen asleep next to me, I wake up needing to pee. Carefully, I slip out of his arms so as not to wake him and make my way to the bathroom. While I'm here, I brush my teeth and stare at myself in the bathroom mirror. I'm still totally naked, and screw it, I look hot. I really do. I've never been so proud of myself in my life. Yet, every time I think something like this, I get over-whelmingly guilty. I feel like some kind of stuck up jerk who is full of herself.

I mean, that's not me. I've always been so self-conscious, so scared of how I look. I've spent three years thinking I'm not good enough for Jace, and three years wishing I was. Now, I sort of feel like the woman he deserves to have sleeping next to him in bed every night. I think back to that stupid reporter calling me a trophy wife. To me, that's an insult meant for a woman who has only one talent— looking good. But, there's nothing wrong with looking good and being a great person as well. That's what my goal is. To be hot in addition to being a great mom and wife.

Then I get an idea, and although it's kind of stupid, I decide to go for it. I sneak back out into our room and grab my phone from my nightstand. Jace is sleeping soundly, his bare chest sexy in our bed. I smile, admiring him for a minute and then I sneak back into the bathroom, closing the door softly behind me.

I use some of the sexy poses they taught me in the photo shoot and snap a few pictures with my phone. It's exhilarating, doing something so naughty, and I find myself flashing back to the last time I'd taken a provocative photo.

I was still living at home and I hadn't met Jace yet. Mom caught me and it was horrifically embarrassing. Of course, that single event led to me being sent away to my grandparents' house and that's where I met Jace. In a way, that stupid photo I took so long ago is the exact reason I am where I am today. It's the reason I'm so happily married, with an awesome kid and a beautiful house. Sometimes really bad screw-ups turn into really good things. So I smile and take another photo.

My plan is to save them for a special occasion and send them to Jace randomly. Maybe while he's working late, or home alone, or when we'll be apart from each other for a while. Maybe even when he's cooking dinner and I'm in the other room working on something, I could send him one of these photos to get his attention. Now that I'm an adult and there's no chance I'll get in trouble by my mom, this is actually fun.

I scroll through the photos, five in all, and try to imagine what Jace will do when he sees them. Then, just for fun, I decide to send one of the photos to Jace's email account at work. He won't see it until he gets to his office tomorrow morning and I'll still be home with Jett. It'll be the perfect surprise.

I open a new email, attach the sexiest photo and type the subject: *Very urgent matter – open ASAP.*

And then I slip back into bed and snuggle up against Jace's back, grinning like crazy.

Being a wife is fun.

CHAPTER 8

On Monday morning, I wake up with an extra pep in my step. Mark had told us the new magazine issue would be out today and I am practically bouncing off the walls as I get dressed and then get Jett dressed and make us breakfast. Actually, I don't make breakfast because I'm too excited. I grab a rice crispy treat and give Jett a bag of Cheerios with his chocolate milk. I figure I can be a bad mom just for today and we'll go back to eating healthy, better breakfasts tomorrow.

Jace and Park are already at the Track when I get there since they arrive ridiculously early to get the track watered and ready to ride. They're both sitting on stools behind the front counter when I walk in with Jett on my hip. Park's wearing a t-shirt and riding pants with flip-flops. They never wear their riding boots inside because they track dirt and mud all over the place.

Jace is still in cargo shorts and a shirt with a black zip-up hoodie. I don't know how he wears shorts when it's like fifty degrees outside, but that's just Jace, I guess. They're drinking coffee and chatting when I walk in. The front desk computer isn't even turned on.

"Is it here?" I ask, wide-eyed and too excited for my own good.

"Is what here?" Park asks, lifting a brow.

"Yeah, what are you talking about?" Jace says.

I put my hand on my hip. Jace cracks first, his confused expression turning into a smile.

"Yeah I can't keep pretending," he says to Park, who rolls his eyes. "We were going to act like we didn't know what you were talking about and make you think the magazine never happened."

"Ya'll are dumb," I say, feeling a blush rise to my cheeks. Of course they would play a prank on me since I've been so ridiculously excited for this stupid magazine. "Well is it here or not?"

I set Jett down on the floor and he runs to his daddy, like he always does. Jace scoops him up and sits him on the counter. I walk over there and give him a quick kiss. Park says, "Eww," under his breath and I punch him in the shoulder.

"Damn, woman, you're getting strong," he says, taking another sip of coffee. "Your punches are actually starting to hurt now."

"Yeah, she's a badass," Jace says, wrapping an arm around me. "Magazine isn't here yet, babe." He pulls me toward him, placing a kiss on top of my hair. "But I don't have a client until ten this morning so I'll hang out here and wait for it with you."

"Awesome," I say, letting my head rest against his shoulder.

A few minutes later, I remember the photo I emailed him last night. A trill of excitement hits me, and I look over at Jace, wondering if he'll mention it while Park is here. But eventually Park leaves for his first client and Jace still hasn't said anything. But the computer is off, so maybe he hasn't checked his office computer, either. I decide to keep my lips closed and wait until he finds it and tells me about it himself.

Jace is talking about his summer camp idea when the front door swings open and we both look over, finding Mark walking inside, his arms full of magazines. My pulse races. I was so freaking excited earlier today and now here I am, frozen in place behind the front counter. I'm almost too scared to read it now.

"Good morning, guys," Mark says, hefting the stack of magazines up and onto the counter. There's probably fifty magazines and they're all shrink-wrapped into a stack. "Fresh off the press," he says, tapping the top of the stack. "It's a good article," he tells me, flashing me a smile. "I wouldn't be surprised if ya'll start getting a ton of new visitors because of it."

"Cool cool," Jace says. He reaches into his pocket and pulls out a pocketknife, then slices open the plastic covering. "Ladies first," he says, handing me the magazine on top.

I gasp. Right there on the cover, is me, standing next to Jace's dirt bike. I'm flashing a look at the camera that's so confident and knowing that I almost don't even recognize myself.

Wives of Motocross it says next to my head. *Bayleigh Adams discusses raising a family, running a business and being married to motocross superstar Jace Adams.*

"You might be more famous than me," Jace says with a grin. He pulls off the shrink wrap and tosses it in the trash. "These babies are going up for everyone to see."

"I have to get going," Mark says, reaching out and shaking our hands. "Thanks so much for being in the article, Bayleigh."

"Thanks for having me," I say, still holding the magazine in my hands. I'm so excited I can't even open the thing yet. I just stare at myself on the cover. I'm on the *cover of a magazine.* I would have never imagined this would happen in a million years.

Eventually I do read the article—well, I try to at least. I end up skimming over it, too excited and freaking out to bother reading each individual sentence. Luckily, Mark was right. The writer only put good things in there, and I'm grateful for it. Becca comes over when her college class is finished and she already has a copy of the magazine in her hand. "Sign it for me?" she says, throwing me a wink.

"Did you read it all?" I ask while I play Legos with Jett. "I've been too scared to actually read it all."

"Yep," she says. "It's all good. No worries."

The front door opens and Jett lets out a squeal and runs toward it. Deja is here for her shift that starts at noon. "Hey little man," she says, waving at Becca and me while she bends down to get on

Jett's level. "Are you ready to play some fun games?"

He nods and shows her his Lego creation.

"Nice magazine article, Mrs. Adams," she says, standing back up with Jett in her arms. "All my friends think its cool as h—" she says, stopping to look at Jett. "Heck," she finishes with a smile. "I mean, you made the cover and everything!"

"I know, I'm excited," I say. "But how did you see it already?"

"Facebook," she says, walking toward the counter to pick up one of the copies. "You're a big deal online."

"What, are you serious?" I ask, almost knocking over Becca in my haste to get to the computer. "It's only been out a few hours."

Deja nods. "It was the first thing I saw on Facebook today. But um, you might want to get Becca to read the comments to you. Don't look at them yourself."

I lift an eyebrow. "What does that mean?"

Becca shoves me out of the way and goes to the internet, pulling up the Track's Facebook page.

Deja bites on her bottom lip. "Well, most of the comments are really nice but you know how people are. Some people are being jerks, but it's rare."

I groan.

"Don't worry about it, Bay," Becca says, her eyes glued to the computer screen. "Here it is. There's two hundred comments already, damn."

I look over, telling myself not to focus on the comments. This morning at seven a.m. Mark posted a picture of the magazine cover to our page. "These aren't so bad," she says, scrolling through comments. I see a bunch of emojis but I don't read any of it. Not until she stops on one particular comment that's typed in all caps.

"What a bitch," she murmurs before she keeps scrolling.

I grab her arm. "No, I want to see it. What was it?"

"Bay, you don't want to see it. I'll just delete it."

"Not until I see what it says," I say, taking the mouse from her. The comment is easy to find and it makes my blood boil.

YEH WHO CARES THIS WOMAN IS A TOTAL SLUT

. . .

THE COMMENT DOESN'T BOTHER ME SO MUCH AS the person who posted it. My teeth grind together. "Natalie," I say, deleting the comment myself. Then I block her from our page. But the act of banning her from commenting doesn't really do anything to help with how angry I am. That bitch tried to ruin my marriage and my life and now she has the nerve to call *me* a slut? Please.

"Do you want me to kick her ass?" Becca says. "Because I'd be happy to. Just say the word, babe."

I shake my head. "If anyone is kicking her ass it'll be me. But I don't think we need to. She's so pathetic." I hold my head up and make a promise to myself that I won't read any more of the comments.

"You're handling this really well," Becca says.

I shrug. "What can I say? I'm on the cover of a magazine and that bitch isn't."

THE DAY PRETTY MUCH FLIES BY AFTER THE magazine is out. I work at the front desk with Becca while Deja keeps Jett in the kid's room. All of our clients see the magazine when they walk in and they all want to talk about it. Many of the teenage riders think it's awesome and ask to take a photo with me to post online. I'm happy to oblige. By the time the work day is over, I'm dying to unwind with a workout in our gym.

Since we opened the gym to up regular memberships, there's already a few guys in here working out when I arrive. I ignore them and head to my favorite weight machine which is a tall cable machine. I slip the metal bar into the fifty-pound weight and turn around to begin my workout.

Only, I can't, because there's a guy standing in front of me. He's lean and muscular, with long dark hair pulled back in a low ponytail. He's wearing a black tight-fitting tank top and sweatpants. I don't recognize him as one of the motocross guys who work out here. He must be someone who signed up for the membership only.

"Hi, can I help you?" I ask, trying to decipher the cryptic look on his face.

"Yeah, sweetheart I think you can," he says, taking a step closer. I back up. My back is very close to the machine, which has two long metal arms on either side. Between it and the guy, I'm kind of boxed in with no way out.

I straighten and try to look fearless. "What the hell does that mean?"

"It means I want more of what I saw online," he says, grinning. His gaze drops down to my chest, where it lingers on my cleavage.

I suppress a shudder. "You mean the magazine article?" Sure, the photos were mildly sexy but they were all about me being a wife. How can he think he can hit on me when he knows I'm married?

The guy shakes his head. "Shit, you're in a magazine, too? I have got to get a copy of it."

Now although he's being creepy as hell, I'm more concerned about what he's talking about than the fact that he's hitting on me. I put my hands on my hips. "What picture are you talking about?"

"The picture you shared on the forums," he says, inching forward. He rests a muscular arm across my machine, blocking me in even more. "I want to see more and something tells me you have more to show."

"Excuse you?" I say, bending to get out of this tight space. "I don't know what the hell you're talking about."

The door slams open behind us and Jace is a welcome sight. His jaw is clenched and he walks with fury. "What the hell are you doing standing so close to my wife?" he growls.

The guy practically leaps backward, holding his

hands up in surrender. "Nah, man, I didn't know she was married. You should keep your girl away from places like this."

"Places like this?" Jace says, giving me a glance to see if I'm okay. "I own this place."

"Okay okay I see," he says, nodding. "I didn't mean to step on any toes. But seriously man, if your wife was so happy with you then you should ask why she spends so much time on the motocross forums."

"I don't even know what you're talking about," I say, finally finding my voice. "I don't go to any forums."

His lips twist into a sneer. "Yeah, probably a good idea to deny in front of your husband over here. Dude looks like he's ready to kill someone."

"Get the hell out of my gym," Jace says.

"I'll get out," he says, though he's looking straight at me. "Of course, you might want to tell your girl here that if she doesn't want attention from guys like me, then maybe she shouldn't post naked pictures of herself online."

CHAPTER 9

Even the walls of Jace's office seem to look down on me as we stare at the computer screen, worried about what we'll see next. After Jace had escorted that jackass out of the building, we'd come into his office to look up these supposed naked photos. I don't feel too worried, not really. I know I didn't post a naked photo of myself on the internet.

I tell Jace this much as he powers up his computer and opens the browser. "It doesn't make any sense," I say, pacing the small space behind his computer chair. "You know I wouldn't do something like that."

"I know, baby," he says, his voice calmer than I feel. "I'm guessing someone photoshopped your head onto a porn star or something. I mean, if that's even what he's talking about. Those magazine photos were a little scandalous, and maybe that's what he was talking about."

"I hope so," I say, sitting on the edge of Jace's desk. "Do you know where to look?"

Jace shakes his head. "He said it was a motocross forum." I watch while he types 'Bayleigh Adams motocross forum' into the browser and searches. The first link that appears makes my blood go cold.

It's a post, dated early this morning. The username who created the post is anonymous but the title says it all.

If you want more where this came from, come see me at the Track! Xoxo

"What the hell?" Jace murmurs, clicking on the link.

"Oh my god!" I slide off the desk and bury my face in my hands. "Oh god, no."

Tears flow immediately and Jace sits there in stunned silence as we stare in horror at the pixels on the screen. It's the photo. It's me.

The one I emailed to Jace last night.

"Bayleigh . . ." Jace's voice is pained. "If you didn't do this, then who did?"

"I—I . . ." the words catch in my throat and I collapse into sobs as I shake my head. There is no way to explain this. No reason why. "I swear I didn't do that," I say. "You have to believe me."

I reach for Jace's hand and he pulls away. His gaze meets mine and there's something beneath his eyes that I've never seen before. Accusation. He runs a hand down his face, the muscle in his jaw flexing. "Bayleigh, who did you take that picture for? It's not some old picture from our past because it's clearly in our new bathroom."

Tears flow from my eyes. It's bad enough to have been so exposed on the freaking internet for the whole world to see. It's another to have your husband look at you with those accusing, heart-broken eyes. "I sent it to you," I say, my voice choked. "Just you."

He lifts an eyebrow. "I've never seen that picture in my life."

"Jace. Yes, you did. I emailed it to you last night." I wipe the tears from my eyes. So many emotions are running through my veins and anger quickly overtakes them. "Don't look at me like that! I swear I only sent it to you."

He shakes his head. "I never got it."

I point toward the computer. "Check your

email. I sent it to your work email and that's all. I swear it was only for you."

He turns back to the computer and opens his email. There's not a single message from me. I draw in a ragged breath, wondering how the hell this could have happened. Did I accidentally send it to someone else instead of Jace? I grab my phone and check, but sure enough, it's right there.

"Look," I say, my hand shaking so bad it makes the phone screen blurry. "I sent it to you last night."

Jace's hand closes over mine. "I believe you babe," he says, sounding resigned. "I never got that email. But someone else clearly did and now they're trying to ruin you."

BECCA RUNS HER HAND OVER MY BACK TRYING TO soothe me but it doesn't really help. As if the events of earlier weren't enough to ruin my day—no, year, now I have to relive all of it with Becca and Park. After the initial shock of seeing my very private photo online, Jace called the owner of the motocross forums, who happens to be his friend. The guy hadn't been online today and therefore never saw the photo. He took it down immediately and blocked the anonymous user that had posted it.

According to the forum, the page had only fifty-three views. Becca uses this statistic over and over again, trying to convince me that it's not that big of a deal. But my rebuttal is always the same: it only takes one person to save the photo and then use it against me for the rest of my life.

Tears fill my eyes again, for the millionth time. Deja's shift was over hours ago, and now although we're at my house in Jace's home office, I really wish she was here. I'm not sure I can handle keeping another human being alive right now when I'm so freaking depressed and humiliated.

Luckily, Jett's bedtime is coming up soon. Right now he's sitting in my lap, and I'm so glad he has no idea what's going on. What if someone keeps this picture and it resurfaces when Jett's a teenager? How humiliated would he be? Would he think less of me?

"Got it," Park says, leaning forward in the computer chair. He's on his own laptop that he brought over. I'd been hesitant to let Park and Becca know about what happened, but Jace insisted. Park's computer skills are apparently a lot better than I'd thought. He grins. "I've traced the

IP address and found the home address of the person who made the post."

My heartbeat quickens. "What are we going to do with this information?"

Jace's eyes meet mine. "We'll report them to the cops."

"We'll screw their shit up," Park says, his lips twisting into an evil grin.

"Okay I like that idea more," I say with a little laugh. It's the first time I've smiled since that guy cornered me in the gym.

Park nods and types more stuff into his computer. "According to the tax records, the owner of this house is just the landlord so someone else rents it. But, that someone else posted their address on an online party invite last weekend." He taps the enter key and a page pops up.

"That witch," Becca seethes. Jace curses under his breath.

My chest explodes in a fury of pain. How is this even possible? My teeth grind together as I stare at the name on the top of the page.

Natalie.

Park swivels in the computer chair, and levels a stare at me. "Bay, are you sure you only sent the photo to Jace's email?"

"Yes," I say for what feels like the millionth time. "I didn't send it anywhere else."

"Is it uploaded to the cloud?"

I shake my head. "No, and I've already checked that, too."

He nods. "Okay then, let me try one more thing . . ."

When he looks up from the computer again, the expression on his face tells me whatever he suspected was true. "Her IP address logged into your work email, Jace. Looks like she's been logging into it every few days. She's been stalking you."

"How the hell is that possible?" Jace says, his knuckles going white. "She doesn't even work with us."

"All she needs is your email address, which is posted on our website, and your password and she can access it from anywhere."

"But how would she get your password?" I ask.

Jace's expression goes from confused to furious in just a few seconds. "I never changed my email password from back when I worked at Mixon," he says slowly, thinking it over. "She probably knew it back then because Mr. Fisher also had my password in case he needed to change my schedule when I wasn't there. She's been stalking me for months."

"For what it's worth, I just trashed her Facebook page," Park says. "And all of her social media pages have been deleted."

"That's a start," Becca says. "But not nearly enough to count as revenge."

"Dammit," Jace says. "Bay? Can you put Jett to bed? I don't want him seeing me like this."

I nod and carry Jett to his room. Becca trails along behind me. "I'll ruin her," she whispers as I place Jett in his crib.

I smile, patting Jett's back and making happy faces at him so he doesn't know anything is wrong. Then, in a soft, pleasing voice so Jett doesn't suspect anything is wrong, I say, "Trust me, I'm going to help you."

"Do you think the cops would do anything about it?" Becca says, petting Jace's blond hair. His eyes get droopy and soon they close.

I shrug. "I don't know. Part of me wants to take care of this in house, if you know what I mean."

"Yeah, I feel that. We'll make her pay."

"But how will we do that without getting in trouble ourselves? The last thing I need is a freaking criminal record."

She considers this a moment, her eyes gazing off into the distance. "I don't know. Park knows some shady people. Maybe we could hire someone."

"I'm not going to have her killed," I say with a snort.

Becca's eyes go wide. "Well no, duh. I mean . . . I don't know. Key her car or something?"

Something happens when I picture Natalie's car being keyed. I think about the look on her face when she walks outside one day and sees something horrible scratched into the shiny paint of her stupid car. What would I choose? *Slut, whore, liar, jealous wench?*

And then it hits me. None of that would make me feel better. Ruining her life wouldn't fix anything. At best, I'd get five seconds of satisfaction before she realizes we did it and turns on me even more. I'd start a war with Natalie and would spend the rest of my life looking over my shoulder out of fear that she's done something to me again.

I watch Jett's chest rise and fall as he drifts off to sleep and something inside of my heart melts. All of the anger and rage at what she's done to me seems to roll up into a ball that I can almost feel inside of me. I close my eyes and toss the ball away.

"No," I say. "I don't want to do any of that. Come on, let's tell the guys."

We head back into the office and Jace and Park are engrossed in talks about how to ruin her life. I hold up my hands and shake my head. "Guys, just stop. Stop thinking of things to do. We removed the picture and Jace changed his email password. That's all we're going to do."

"What? Why?" Jace and Park talk at the same time.

I glance at Becca and see understanding in her eyes. I draw in a deep breath and let it out slowly. "It's just not worth it. She's the jealous one here, not me. I feel bad for her. She's so jealous and hateful that she's been stalking you for months just to finally find something to use against me. That's her problem, not mine."

Everyone stares at me silently and I focus on Jace. "I won't let my friends and myself turn into vengeful, spiteful people just because of one stupid thing she did. We are all better than that."

Becca takes my hand and squeezes it. Jace's lips form a thin smile. "If that's what you want to do, babe, then we'll support it."

I nod. "Yeah, that's what I want to do."

CHAPTER 10

As the days roll by, I'm feeling more confident about my decision not to backlash at Natalie for what she'd done to me. Luckily, after that incident with the guy at the gym, no one has said anything else about the picture. I'm not sure if it's because no one I know in person actually saw it, or if they're just being polite. Regardless, I hold my head high and I work as hard as I can at the Track and I get on with my life.

It feels good to let it go. To just go on with my life and forget about people who are going to hate me no matter what. Natalie would have never been my friend. I can't let that bother me.

Jace's friend who owns the forums had assured us that something like that would never happen again. He'd set up some kind of filter so that no one could post a photo without it being approved first. That was really cool of him and it just goes to show how much influence Jace has over people. They really like him and they're always happy to help him out.

I hope that one day, I'll have those kinds of friends as well.

"I was thinking we should take a vacation soon," Jace says one Friday evening when we're finally home from a long day at work. He's grilling hotdogs for dinner so Jett and I are hanging out on the patio with him.

"A vacation?" I say, watching Jett play in his sandbox. "You mean being married to me isn't enough of a vacation for you?" I give him a playful smile.

He closes the lid on the grill and walks over to me, taking a seat in the patio chair next to me. "I think we should go somewhere as a family. It doesn't have to be some crazy thing, just like hit up Sandals in Jamaica or something."

"Only you would think flying to another country and staying at a resort isn't that big of a deal."

He reaches for a beer from the cooler and

cracks the lid, then hands it to me and gets another one for himself.

I take a sip and throw my head back, staring up at the twilight sky. "I could go for a vacation. Do you think Jett would be good in an airplane?"

"We'll fly at night and I'm sure he'll be fine. Won't you, little man?"

Jett just grins and tosses his toy dirt bike into the sand.

"Now that I'm thinking about it, a vacation sounds kind of awesome," I say, letting thoughts of warm white sand and clear blue water fill my daydreams. "You work so hard babe. You totally deserve the break."

"I wasn't suggesting a vacation for me," he says, reaching out and brushing the hair from my face. "You work harder than anyone around here. You run the business, you take care of Jett and somehow our house is always clean." He tucks a strand of loose hair behind my ear and then his fingers graze along my cheek. I still get butterflies in my stomach when he looks at me like his. "I was suggesting a vacation for you. You deserve to just chill and be lazy for a while."

I reach for his hand and hold it to my face. His

touch feels so perfect, so right. "Do you think Park can handle the place without us?" I ask.

He shrugs and takes another sip from his beer. "Only one way to find out."

"So, March first," I say, dropping onto my side of the bed. A giddy feeling rushes through me as I look over the booking papers I just printed out. "We're totally going to Jamaica. I can't believe this."

"Believe it," Jace says. "I can't believe it only takes twenty minutes to book a two-week trip to another country. When my baby knows what she wants, she definitely knows how to get it."

"Yup," I say, sticking out my tongue. After we'd eaten and put Jett to bed, Jace and I got online and ordered a reservation to the beautiful island resort. It's an all-inclusive trip and it's all booked and waiting for us to show up. I can't freaking wait. I'm going to look so hot in a bikini this year.

He stands in the closet doorway, wearing nothing but a pair of dark blue boxers. He towels off his short hair and grins at me. I could watch him dry off for hours, if only it took that long. I love the look of his biceps going taunt as he moves the towel around his head. There's something incredibly sexy about a guy getting out of the shower.

Or maybe that's just Jace. Everything is sexy about him.

"There's something I've been meaning to tell you," he says as he walks back to the bathroom to hang up his towel.

"Oh yeah?" I sit up in bed, pulling my knees up to my chest. Something in the way he says it makes my stomach hurt. Things were going so well lately —I don't really want to talk about anything serious right now.

As if sensing my trepidation, Jace's features soften. "It's nothing bad." He moves closer to the bed and then sits next to me. "I never got a chance to comment on that picture you emailed me."

"Oh, Jace. We're past this," I say with a groan. Things are finally back to normal and the last thing I want to talk about is that stupid naked picture incident.

"No, I meant the picture itself." He runs a hand through his hair and then turns to me, giving me a sultry gaze. "It was really sexy."

I give him a sheepish grin, but it's hard to be

happy about it when the topic is still such a fresh wound to my spirit. "I'm glad you liked it," I say, staring at my hands. "I took a few more but now I'm too scared to send them."

"It would have been a nice surprise, had I actually gotten the email."

I nod, still unable to meet his eyes. When I think about the picture I think about seeing it on that stupid website. The scent of Jace's body wash overwhelms me as he inches closer to me on the bed, his knees touching mine as we face each other. He reaches for my hands, pulls them out of my lap and into his lap.

"I *love* you," he says in a sing-song.

I meet his gaze and his eyes are twinkling. "I'm sorry about everything that happened. You can't let it break you."

"I'm not," I say, squeezing his hands. "I'd just rather not talk about it. It's behind me and I'd rather never think about it again."

"Yeah, that's why I haven't brought it up. Talking about that picture makes us think of the . . . event . . . surrounding it. But I just wanted to say that I have the hottest wife on earth and I am so lucky."

He wiggles his eyebrows suggestively. It makes me laugh and then that makes him laugh. He leans in and wraps his arms around my shoulders, pulling me in for a hug. "I love you so much."

"I love you, too, you dork."

He runs a hand through my hair and gazes down at me. "Dorky or not, I mean it. I love you so much, Bay. More than anyone has ever loved anyone."

"You seem pretty confident in that," I tease, running my fingers down his bare chest.

"It's easy to be confident when you're right." When he brushes his lips against my neck I close my eyes and let the sensation take over all of my nerve endings.

"You are my favorite person," I whisper, turning to meet his lips.

"You know I'm always here for you," Jace says, taking my face in his hands. He tilts my head to look up at him and when my eyes meet his, I feel the intensity of his gaze. "There will always be shitty people in life, babe. We just have to appreciate the good and roll with the bad. You know I'm always here for you. Always."

I close my eyes and lean into him, letting my head rest on his shoulder. After everything we've been through already and everything we will go through in the future, I know we'll make it just fine. Jace is my soulmate and we will always be there for each other. "I know," I say, feeling the warmth of our love spread across my heart. "Always."

NOTE FROM THE AUTHOR

I'd like to extend a HUGE thank you to everyone who has read this far. It means you picked up Summer Unplugged and felt compelled to finish the series. Thank you so much. Ten books are a lot, even if most of them are novellas, and I am so truly grateful to have you as a reader.

I started writing Summer Unplugged as a "fun" exercise when my brain was too muddled with stress and other crap to try writing the other project I was working on. I had an idea about a girl who gets her whole summer ruined by being grounded from her phone. I worked on it for fun, late into the night, and it was my way to escape real life. I didn't think it would go anywhere, because at the time it was just a novella and I was under the impression that no one read short books. Then, one day when I was thinking about taking the indie publishing route, I made up this fake name for myself and published Summer Unplugged just as an experiment. I wanted to see how publishing worked, and I used a story I thought everyone would overlook. This was just an experiment to see how publishing worked, after all.

To my surprise, Summer Unplugged started selling a few copies a day. And I hadn't even told anyone. Then the sales increased and emails started coming in. I remember reading emails from people like Krissy Stanton (hey girl!) asking me if I'd write a sequel. It was the coolest request ever, and I happily wrote three more books. Then I wrote another, and another, and well, you know how the story goes. Jace and Bayleigh are more than just people in my head now, they are a part of your life, too. After three years, the series is complete at ten books and I hope I've made you all proud.

I never expected to be embraced by such a great group of readers. You guys keep me going during the dark times of writing and your emails always brighten my day. Thank you so much for your continued support.

THE SUMMER UNPLUGGED SERIES

Part 1 - Summer Unplugged

Part 2 - Autumn Unlocked

Part 3 - Winter Untold

Part 4 - Spring Unleashed

Part 5 - The Beginning of Forever

Part 6 - Autumn Adventure

Part 7 - Winter Wonderful

Part 8 - The Girl with my Heart

Part 9 - Autumn Awakening

Part 10 - Winter Whirlwind

Part 11 - Unplugged Summer

Don't miss all of the spin-off series:

The Summer Series

The Believe in Love Series

The Team Loco Series

The Love on the Track Series

The Love at the Gym Series

The Summer Unplugged Epilogues

ABOUT THE AUTHOR

Amy Sparling is the *USA Today* bestselling author of books for teens and the teens at heart. She lives on the coast of Texas with her family, her spoiled rotten pets, and a huge pile of books. She graduated with a degree in English and has worked at a bookstore, coffee shop, and a fashion boutique. Her fashion skills aren't the best, but luckily she turned her love of coffee and books into a writing career that means she can work in her pajamas. Her favorite things are coffee, book boyfriends, and Netflix binges.

She started writing her own books in 2010 and now publishes several books a year. She also writes young adult and middle grade novels under the name Cheyanne Young.

Connect with her on at AmySparling.com

www.ingramcontent.com/pod-product-compliance
Lightning Source LLC
Chambersburg PA
CBHW031753150726
47989CB00006B/2702